James David Edgar

This Canada of Ours and Other Poems

James David Edgar

This Canada of Ours and Other Poems

ISBN/EAN: 9783744770293

Printed in Europe, USA, Canada, Australia, Japan

Cover: Foto ©Andreas Hilbeck / pixelio.de

More available books at **www.hansebooks.com**

THIS CANADA OF OURS

AND OTHER POEMS.

BY

J. D. EDGAR, M.P.

TORONTO:
WILLIAM BRIGGS, WESLEY BUILDINGS.
Montreal: C. W. Coates. | Halifax: S. F. Huestis.
1893.

CONTENTS.

*

THIS CANADA OF OURS.

A NATIONAL SONG.

LET other tongues in older lands
Loud vaunt their claims to glory,
And chaunt in triumph of the past,
Content to live in story.
Tho' boasting no baronial halls,
Nor ivy-crested towers,
What past can match thy glorious youth,
Fair Canada of ours?
Fair Canada,
Dear Canada,
This Canada of ours!

We love those far-off ocean Isles,
Where Britain's monarch reigns;

We'll ne'er forget the good old blood
  That courses through our veins;
Proud Scotia's fame, old Erin's name,
  And haughty Albion's powers,
Reflect their matchless lustre on
      This Canada of ours.
          Fair Canada,
          Dear Canada,
      This Canada of ours!

May our Dominion flourish then,
  A goodly land and free,
Where Celt and Saxon, hand in hand,
  Hold sway from sea to sea;
Strong arms shall guard our cherished homes,
  When darkest danger lowers,
And with our life-blood we'll defend
      This Canada of ours.
          Fair Canada,
          Dear Canada,
      This Canada of ours!

KESWICK BAY,

To — — — — —

O come from your briefs and your office,
  Break loose from those fetters to-day,
For sweet as the breath of the Summer
  Are the breezes of Keswick Bay,

That play o'er its sky-blue water,
  And the changeful greens of its shore,
As we glide to the dip of the paddle,
  Or fly to the sweep of the oar.

7

From the breezy hill where the pine-trees
  Are sighing their fragrance away,
I'll show you the wavelets sparkle,
  And the dancing zephyrs at play.

And after the storm-clouds gather,
  That sweep over Oro's hill,
I'll show you the waves of shadow
  On the meadows of Innisfil.

We'll sail to Ke-nah-bec Island,
  Where the last of the O-jib-way
Will tell us the ancient legends
  Of the Red man and Keswick Bay;

Of the great black-crested serpent
  With eyes of fiery red,
That dwelt in the Holland marshes,
  And hid in the river's bed,

And prowl'd abroad in the darkness,
  The terror of lake and land,

Till it came to Ke-nah-bec Island,
    And perish'd by Esquib's hand.

When sunset is bursting in splendour,
    And dyeing the west with its glare,
And burning the waters with crimson,
    And flashing red darts through the air,

We'll bring our good craft to an anchor
    Near a shore where the white birches shine :
Look out ! or your rod will be broken,
    A black bass is fast on your line !

He plunges and dashes in fury—
    Let him have all the line he will take,
Till the landing-net holds him securely—
    A four-pounder—king of the lake.

And after our basket is heavy,
    Sailing back by the light of the moon,
As we round up our yacht at her moorings
    We hear the sad call of the loon,

Like a wail of distress from the water;
The night-hawk replies from the hill,
And there floats from a far-away thicket
The plaint of the lone whip-poor-will.

The sunset has melted in silver,
The crimsons have faded to grey,
And softly, in silence and shadow,
Night falls on the beautiful bay.

CANADIAN AUTUMN TINTS.

WE wandered off together,
  We walked in dreamful ease,
In mellow autumn weather,
  Past autumn-tinted trees ;
The breath of soft September
  Left fragrance in the air,
And well do I remember,
  I thought you true as fair.

The maples' deep carnations,
  The beeches' silv'ry sheen,
Hid nature's sad mutations,
  And I forgot the green :

11

Forgot the green of summer,
  The buds of early spring,
And gave the latest comer
  My false heart's offering.

O painted autumn roses !
O dying autumn leaves !
Your beauty fades and closes,
  That gaudy hue deceives :
Like clouds that gather golden
  Around the setting sun,
Your glories are beholden
  Just ere the day is done.

Or, like th' electric flushes
  That fire Canadian skies,
Your bright and changeful blushes
  In gold and crimson rise.
But health has long departed
  From all that hectic glare ;

And love sees, broken-hearted,
   The fate that's pictured there.

The brush that paints so brightly
   No mortal artist wields ;
He touches all things lightly,
   But sweeps the broadest fields.
The fairest flowers are chosen
   To wither at his breath ;
The hand is cold and frozen
   That paints those hues of death.

We wandered back together,
   With hearts but ill at ease,
In mellow autumn weather,
   Past autumn-tinted trees ;
The breath of soft September
   Left fragrance in the air,
And well we both remember
   The love that ended there.

AROUSE YE, BRAVE CANADIANS!

Lines suggested by General Brock's stirring appeal to the people of Upper Canada at the opening of the War of 1812.

CANADIAN arms are stout and strong,
  Canadian hearts are true;
Your homes were in the forest made,
  Where pine and maple grew.
A haughty foe is marching
  Your country to enthral;
Arouse ye, brave Canadians,
  And answer to my call!

Let every man who swings an axe,
　Or follows at the plough,
Abandon farm and homestead,
　And grasp a rifle now!
We'll trust the God of Battles,
　Although our force be small;
Arouse ye, brave Canadians,
　And answer to my call!

Let mothers, though with breaking hearts,
　Give up their gallant sons;
Let maidens bid their lovers go,
　And wives their dearer ones!
Then rally to the frontier,
　And form a living wall;
Arouse ye, brave Canadians,
　And answer to my call!

THE CANADIAN SONG SPARROW.

(See Note 1.)

From the leafy maple ridges,
From the thickets of the cedar,
From the alders by the river,
From the bending willow branches,
From the hollows and the hillsides,
Through the lone Canadian forest,
Comes the melancholy music,
Oft repeated, never changing—
  "All—is—vanity—vanity—vanity."

16

Where the farmer ploughs his furrow,
Sowing seed with hope of harvest,
In the orchards, white with blossom,
In the early fields of clover,
Comes the little brown-clad singer,
Flitting in and out of bushes,
Hiding well behind the fences,
Piping forth his song of sadness,
  " Poor—hu—manity—manity—manity."

B

CANADIAN CAMPING SONG.

A WHITE tent pitched by a glassy lake,
  Well under a shady tree,
Or by rippling rills from the grand old hills,
  Is the summer home for me.
I fear no blaze of the noontide rays,
  For the woodland glades are mine,
The fragrant air, and that perfume rare,
  The odour of forest pine.

CHORUS.

The wild woods, the wild woods,
  The wild woods give me;
The wild woods of Canada,
  The boundless and free!

A cooling plunge at the break of day,
  A paddle, a row, or sail,
With always a fish for a mid-day dish,
  And plenty of Adam's ale.
With rod or gun, or in hammock swung,
  We glide through the pleasant days ;
When darkness falls on our canvas walls,
  We kindle the camp-fire's blaze.

From out the gloom sails the silv'ry moon,
  O'er forests dark and still,
Now far, now near, ever sad and clear,
  Comes the plaint of whip-poor-will ;
With song and laugh, and with kindly chaff,
  We startle the birds above,
Then rest tired heads on our cedar beds,
  To dream of the ones we love.

UN CANADIEN ERRANT.

(See Note 2.)

Un Canadien errant,
Banni de ses foyers,   }*(bis.)*

Parcourait en pleurant
Des pays étrangers.   }*(bis.)*

Un jour, triste et pensif,
Assis au bord des flots,   }*(bis.)*

Au courant fugitif,
Il adressa ces mots ;   }*(bis.)*

20

A CANADIAN EXILE.

A TRANSLATION.

EXILED and wandering
From his Canadian home,

It breaks his bleeding heart
In distant lands to roam.

One day in grief he sate
Beside the western wave,

And to its fleeting flood
These solemn words he gave:

21

" Si tu vois mon pays,
Mon pays malheureux.   }*(bis.)*

" Va, dis à mes amis,
Que je me souviens d'eux.   }*(bis.)*

" O jours si pleins d'appas,
Vous êtes disparus . . . . }*(bis.)*

" Et ma patrie, hélas !
Je ne la verrai plus !   }*(bis.)*

" Non, mais en expirant,
O mon cher Canada !   }*(bis.)*

" Mon regard languisant
Vers toi se portera. . . ." }*(bis.)*

" If you see my country,
That dear, unhappy land,

" Tell every loving friend
That I would clasp his hand.

" O past days of delight,
I think of you in vain,

" And my best loved country
I ne'er shall see again !

" But in my dying hour,
Wherever I may be,

" O Canada, my home,
Mine eyes shall turn to thee ! "

ON THE SAGUENAY.

"IMPROMPTU."

From the French of Louis H. Fréchette, in "*Pêle-Mêle.*"

THE forest has spells to enchant me,
   The mountain has power to enthral :
Yet the grace of a wayside blossom
   Can stir my heart deeper than all.

O towering steeps, that are mirrored
   On Saguenay's darkening breast !
O grim, rocky heights, sternly frowning,
   The thunders have smitten your crest !

24

O sentinels, piercing the cloudland,
  Stand forth in stupendous array!
My brow, by your shadows enshrouded,
  Is humbled before you to-day.

But, peaks that are gilded by heaven,
  Defiant you stand in your pride!
From glories too distant above me,
  I turn to the friend by my side.

A SUMMER NIGHT.

NUIT D'ÉTÉ.

————

From the French of Fréchette, in Pêle Mêle.

————

WE wandered together, Louise, and you knew
That the dreams of my heart were tender and
true.

Silent and calm was the midsummer night,
Our dreams grew more dazzling, as faded the
light.
What echoes are filling the solitudes vast,

26

What sounds are those floating on wings of
   the blast?
The Spirits of Midnight are chaunting the
   words,
The wind of the desert is striking the chords.
The meteors of heaven illumine the sky,
And the voice of the pine tree is lost in a sigh.
From nests in the branches, the fond turtle-
   doves
Are warbling to heaven their infinite loves.

We wandered together, Louise, all the way,
And surely you knew what my heart had to
   say.

The night air was stirring, it rustled the trees,
Our foreheads were fanned by the scent-laden
   breeze,
Which sprinkled the dew-drops o'er meadow
   and lea,
And crept o'er the lakelet, to die in the sea.

No sleep for our eyelids—we roam in delight,
And weave in a garland the hours of the
night.
O joys of the moment! too fleeting you seem,
The soul is in cloudland, the mind in a dream.
As the fire of youth kindles, and breaks into
flame,
What harmonies waken, and thrill through my
frame.

We wandered together, Louise, all along;
You echoed my heart when it murmured in
song.

Where a cloudlet comes sailing through ether
serene
The moon bursts in glory and silvers the
scene.
Though voices of lovers are whispering low,
The Angel of Parting commands us to go;
For happiness stays but an hour from its birth,

And pleasures, so perfect, are not for this
  earth.
The moments are fleeting, we falter and sigh,
Our hearts are both broken, for parting is
  nigh ;
With pledges and kisses we mingle our vows,
When breezes of morning are stirring the
  boughs.

You are gone, my Louise ; will you ever forget
The sighs at our parting, the joys when we
  met ?

NUNC EST BIBENDUM.

TRANSLATION.

Now drink and dance, my comrades,
   And spread the splendid feast,
The haughty Queen of Egypt
   Is fleeing to the East.

When Cæsar led his war-ships,
   Spread far in battle line,
A panic fell upon her,
   Half mad with lust and wine.

She fled before his galleys
 Far from the Italian shore;
The herd of loathsome traitors
 Now threaten Rome no more.

As swoops the eagle on the dove,
 The hunter on the hare,
So Cæsar followed swiftly
 To bind her in her lair.

The daughter of a hundred kings,
 She spurned the Roman chains,
And sought to spill the fiery blood
 That swelled her ruby veins.

She failed ! but in her woman's breast
 Her courage rose serene;
She walked again her father's halls,
 And still was Egypt's queen.

She pictured the proud triumph
Beneath the Roman sky,
And fiercely flamed her passion,
And sternly flashed her eye ;

In her ears the chariots rumbled,
In her ears the shoutings rang,
Then she bared her snowy bosom
To the serpent's poisoned fang.

THE GREAT DIVIDE.

AN ACROSTIC.

(See Note 3.)

---

*T*wo little rain drops side by side
*H*ere at the top of the Great Divide,
*E*ver while falling their love grows warm,
*G*rows as they drift in the arms of the storm.
*R*estless they float where the wild winds fly,
*E*arthward they gaze from the cloudland high,
*A*imless no longer they rush below,
*T*winkling their eyes in the sunset glow,
*D*own to the flowers, the rivers and trees,
*I*nto the paths of the summer breeze,
*V*owing to wander together for aye,
*I*nto the fatal divide they stray ;
*D*ivided for ever they float along,
*E*ach sings to the other a parting song.

c
33

THE WHITE STONE CANOE.

A LEGEND OF THE OTTAWAS.

(See Note 4.)

DARK and solemn stand the pine trees,
And the hemlock casts its shadows,
Where the forest spreads unbroken
From the Great Lake of the Hurons,
To the Lakes of many Islands,
To the waters of Muskoka.

All the voices of the woodland,
All the music of the waters,

Every whisper of the breezes,
Stirred the blood of young Abeka,
When he wandered with his Wabose,
Through the shadows of that forest,
In the fulness of the summer,
Breathing words of love and gladness.

O the dreary days of autumn,
When he watched her sinking, dying,
Flushed with fever like the maple,
Shaken like the leaves of aspen.
Ere the early snows of winter
Spread their mantle o'er the forest,
She had passed to the Hereafter.
Kindly hands of women bore her
To her distant place of burial,
Where the tall and stately pine trees
Tower above the birch and basswood.

There Abeka often lingered,
Catching echoes from the branches

Of his sighing and his moaning,
When the North winds played upon them.

Through the gloom of frozen forests,
When the snow lay on the branches,
Bending down the longest branches
Of the hemlock and the cedar,
All alone Abeka wandered,   .
For his heart was dead within him.
Lonely were his midnight watchings,
Startled by the night owl's screeching,
Or the shrill and dismal music
Of the wolfish pack approaching.
Sometimes silent hours of moonlight
Shed their magic o'er the forest.
And the rabbit, the Wabasso—
Little white one, like the maiden—
Leaped along its beaten pathways,
Paused, and full of timid wonder,
Fixed its two soft eyes upon him.

In the lodges of his people,
Never had been seen a Pale-Face;
Never yet had come a Black Robe
Bearing Cross of mystic meaning.
Only vague and blind traditions,
Only secrets of magicians,
Empty songs and incantations,
Taught him of the world of spirits
Of the land of the Hereafter.

Though he well had loved the war-path,
And was proud of skill in hunting,
Bow and arrows lay neglected,
In those heavy days of anguish.
But one thought was ever with him,
But one wild desire possessed him;
For the old men often told him,
That by fasting and by dreaming,
By forsaking all his kindred,
By forgetting all his prowess,
He might find the hidden pathway

To the land of Souls and Shadows.
This one purpose fired his fancy;
Daily fasts and nightly vigils
Gave him weird and mystic visions,
Filling all his mind with wonder,
Hope and wonder, strangely blended.

Rising with the sun one morning,
Followed by his faithful deer-hound,
Over frozen lakes and rivers,
Over swamps and over mountains,
Guided by the old traditions,
With light feet he started Southward.
Though the air were thick with snow-flakes,
Though the sun and stars were hidden,
Yet he never was mistaken,
Never took the wrong direction,
For the topmost boughs of hemlock
Bent before the fierce North-west wind,
Pointed with unerring finger,
To the South-east always pointed.

Snowshoes, made with thongs of deerskin,
Tightly stretched on frames of hardwood,
Bore him lightly over snowdrifts,
Marking all his path behind him ;
Till the sunshine, growing stronger,
Melted every trace of winter.
And he heard the sweet birds singing,
Saw the fragrant blossoms bursting,
And the tender leaflets shewing
Tips of green on all the branches.
Now Abeka's footsteps quickened,
For he saw a well worn pathway
Through a grove of giant pine trees—
Just as promised by traditions,
Old traditions of his people,
Coming from the distant ages,
When the souls of the departed
Held communion still with mortals.

Silently he followed onward,
Through the melancholy pine trees,

With their sad and solemn swaying,
And their sighing in the South wind.
Save the sighing of the pine trees,
All was perfect stillness round him.
Many times he saw a White Dove
Flitting through the deepest shadows,
Noiseless as the sailing cloudlet,
Shining out against the darkness,
Whiter than the snows of winter.

Soon he found the path ascending,
Till he reached a lofty terrace,
Near the summit of a mountain.
What is this he now encounters!
What strange vision so appals him!

Once before, when wounded, bleeding,
Tortured by his cruel foemen,
While they sang the death-song o'er him,
He had seen the dreadful Paw-guk,

Waiting for him in the darkness—
Now again he sees him waiting.

Clad in robes of blackest sable,
At a wigwam's open doorway,
Stood a form of giant stature ;
Hoary locks in snowy whiteness
Floated, cloudlike, down his shoulders ;
Fiercely burned his fiery eyeballs,
Piercing through Abeka's bosom,
Reading every thought within him.

Fear, at first, had made him speechless,
Hope soon filled his heart with boldness,
And, in words of power and passion,
He began to tell his story.
Scarce ten rapid words were spoken,
When the other interrupted :—

" Cease your idle talk of these things,
" For I know your thoughts and actions,

" Know your passion and your sorrow ;
" I have helped you on this journey,
" I am here to bid you welcome.
" She, whom you are seeking after,
" Rested with me, way worn, weary,
" Rested for her journey onward.
" Enter now into my wigwam,
" I will answer your enquiries,
" Give you guidance for the future."

Kindly, then, he led Abeka,
Seated him on couch of bearskin,
Answered all his eager questions,
Told him when his Wabose passed there,
How she urgently entreated
That she might return to wander
Through the forests near Abeka,
With the birds to warble to him,
With the winds to breathe upon him ;
Sometimes, in his dreams to tell him
All the love she lavished on him.

Sadly had she learned the lessons
Of her altered state and nature,
Of her future life and duties.
But one answer she had offered
To all words of hope and promise—
" Happiness comes not without him,
" Joy is only in his presence,
" I will wait till he comes for me—
" Send and tell him I am waiting."

Then the Master of the Wigwam,
Taking pity on her sorrow,
Called his messenger, the White Dove,
Told her—if she found Abeka
Bearing equal love for Wabose,
From the land of snows to bring him.

Thus Abeka learned the secret
Of those weird and mystic visions,
That had filled his mind with wonder—
Hope and wonder, strangely blended.

And he heard, with deep emotion,
Why the White Dove hovered round him,
In his fasts and in his vigils,
Stirred his thoughts, and shaped his fancies,
Till she led him through the forest,
Toward the land of Souls and Shadows.
These things all were told Abeka
By the Master of the Wigwam.

Then he took Abeka with him,
Out again, and pointing Southward,
" Yonder lake," he said, " divides you
" From the land of Souls and Shadows.
" Standing here you see its borders,
" You may view its plains of verdure,
" And the sparkling of its waters,
" And the purple of its mountains.
" But you cannot take your body ;
" Leave it with your bow and arrows,
" Leave it with your dog and knapsack ;
" On returning you shall find them."

Quick compliance made Abeka,
And upon a couch of bearskin
Left his body, still and lifeless,
Guarded by his faithful deer-hound. .

Thrilling with a sense of freedom,
Bounding forward like a red deer,
Sweeping onward like an eagle,
Like an arrow flew Abeka.
Forests, rivers, glens and mountains,
All were there; but greater beauty
Clothed the face of hill and valley,
Brighter blossoms decked the woodland,
Birds he saw of rarest plumage,
All the beasts had lost their shyness—
Timid fawns seemed not to fear him.

As the sun shines through the water,
As the sea gull sails the storm wind,
As the moonbeams pierce the forest,
So Abeka smoothly glided,

Like a shadow among shadows,
Onward through the trees and branches.

Thus, for half a day he journeyed,
And the landscape grew more varied—
Richer in its changing beauty,
Fairer than his brightest visions.
Then he saw the shining water
Of a broad lake spread before him.
Bending branches fringed the margin,
Casting shadows on the pebbles;
Swans and wild fowl sailed upon it,
Rising, falling, with the billows,
While, below them, golden fishes
Swam and glistened in the sunlight.

In the distance rose an Island—
Clad with verdure all its mountains,
Bright with blossom all its valleys.
Floating on the crystal waters,
A canoe of dazzling whiteness,

Fashioned out of purest White Stone,
Waited, ready for Abeka.
Stepping lightly in the centre,
Scarcely had he touched a paddle,
When he turned and saw beside him
His dear Wabose, his long lost one,
With her own canoe and paddle,
White and shining like the other.

She restrained his strong emotion
By her smiles and warning gestures.
Shining from her lovely features
Glowed a radiancy of beauty,
Pure and gentle as the moonlight,
Clear and sparkling as the starlight.
By her loving smile he knew her,
By her eyes that oft had spoken
More than falt'ring tongue could tell him.
Then she, pointing towards the Island,
Signed to him to hasten thither.
Imitating all his motions,

By his side she paddled onward
Out upon the limpid waters.

Soon the waves rose up before them
Curling, dark and fierce, upon them,
Threat'ning both canoes with danger.
As the white canoes approached it,
Every billow seemed to vanish,
Fading as they glided through it,
Melting like the mist of morning.
For the Master of Life remembered
That their lives had both been blameless.
He had helped the old and feeble,
Many times he shared their burdens,
Fed them through the dreary winters,
Giving from his corn and venison—
Fruits of hunting and of labour—
She had cared for little children,
Tenderly had loved the orphans,
Nursed the wounds of stricken warriors,
And had often wept and pleaded,

Begging mercy for the captives
That they might be spared from torture.

But the sights of that strange voyage
Filled the lovers' hearts with sorrow.
Fathoms deep, beneath the water,
Strewn upon the sandy reaches,
Scatter'd o'er the rocky ledges,
Lay the forms of those who perished
On their passage towards the Island.

All around them in the waters,
Old and young were struggling, sinking,
Men and maidens without number,
Of all nations, tribes and kindreds.
Ancient chiefs and famous warriors,
Came with shouts of hope and triumph,
Dashed their paddles through the surges,
Laughing at the foaming billows.
Vain were all their fierce exertions,
Useless all their foolish shouting ;

D

No one listened to their clamour,
None applauded at their boasting.
Slowly each canoe was filling,
Sinking lower, sinking surely,
Unless hidden hands of Spirits
Smoothed its pathway through the waters.
Guardian Spirits these, who follow
·Each of us from days of childhood,
Ready always with assistance,
Anxious always to befriend us.
But their power to help is measured
By the love we bear our fellows,
By the kindness of our actions,
And our sympathy for sorrow.

On this passage to the Island
There were some canoes of White Stone
Bearing only little children—
· Happy, smiling little children—
And the waters never harmed them,

As they glided gently onwards,
To the Island of the Blessed.

Suddenly, as in a moment,
After passing through all dangers,
On the shore the two companions
Found themselves in safety landed.
Hand in hand they went together,
Over flowery fields they wandered;
Through the glades of leaf and blossom,
Where the waterfalls made music,
Where the streamlet softly murmured,
Sending to the birds above it
Songs to match their sweetest singing.
All the fragrance of the woodland,
All the beauties of the forest,
All its charms and all its secrets,
Filled their hearts with joy unspoken.
Cold and famine came not near them,
For the balmy air sustained them,
And they quaffed the spicy South wind.

There, on couch of moss reclining,
Long they watched the Souls and Shadows,
Thronging past in countless numbers,
Turning gentle eyes upon them,
Wearing each a smile of gladness,
Giving looks of love and welcome.
All remembrance of the sorrows,
Of the troubles and the sadness
In the old life of the mortals,
Had been swept from out their mem'ries
By the fierce and stormy waters.
And no voice of lamentation,
And no words of pain or anguish,
And no bitter cry of parting,
Broke the peaceful stillness round them.

When the actions in the old life
Had been cruel, false, and selfish,
And the beating of the storm waves
Could not wash away their traces
From the memories of the Shadows,

These could never reach the Island,
But forlorn, forsaken beings,
To and fro they ever drifted,
With the currents and the tempests,
Till, at last, they sank to silence,
In the sleep that is eternal.

While Abeka mused and pondered
On the mystery of his new life,
Came a voice of softest cadence,
Floating on the gentle breezes,
Floating like a cloud in summer.
Though the accents thrilled Abeka,
And he knew their fullest meaning,
Yet the words were not a language
Spoken by the Earthly nations.

All around they felt a Presence,
In the shadows It was near them,
In the sunlight It was with them,
But their eyes could not behold It.

As the mother stills her infant,
By her sweet but wordless singing ;
As the wild bird sounds her warning
To the timid brood around her,
So the Voice that reached Abeka
Spoke to him with fullest meaning,
" Go," it said, " back to your people,
" Since your task is not accomplished.
" To your people I will send you,
" You shall be a chief among them,
" Ruling them with love and wisdom.
" For great purposes I made you—
" These my messenger shall show you
" When he gives you back your body,
" So that you may guide your people,
" So that you may lead them with you,
" Safely to the Happy Island.
" Go, but leave your Wabose with me ;
" She shall wait your second coming,
" Always young and always faithful,

" Young and fair as when I called her
" From the land of snows and forests."

When, in after years, Abeka
Told the story of this journey
To the listeners in his Wigwam,
Sometimes doubters were among them,
Who believed that in his fasting,
In his long and weary vigils,
He had seen a mystic vision,
And had never left his body,
Never crossed the stormy water,
Never seen again his Wabose.

But none ever dared to show him
That they doubted what he told them :
For he faithfully believed it ;
And he ruled his people wisely,
So that he might take them with him,
When he next should cross the water,
In the bright canoe of White Stone,
To the Island of the Blessed.

EUTHANASY.

The weary brain cries out for rest—
  An end to hopes, an end to fears,
  An end to hours and days and years,
An end to time itself were best.
  The soul breathes out her litany—
To sleep in peace, to leave the light,
  To sink in silent lethargy,
And glide beyond the gates of night
  On wings of soft Euthanasy.

What voices pierce the ether clear?
  From distant stars they seem to roll,
  The answer of the Over-Soul;
Their music murmurs in the ear
  Like whisperings of eternity.
They call us back to Nature's breast,
  To end life's awful mystery,
And dream in the eternal rest
  That comes beyond Euthanasy.

THE THISTLE OF SCOTLAND.

(Written for the Caledonian Society of Toronto.)

GIVE France her flaunting *fleur-de-lis*,
England her damask rose;
Let Ireland love the triple leaf
That on her greensward blows.

The land that nurtured Robert Bruce,
Where Wallace won his name,
Must find a sterner emblem flower
To symbol Scotland's fame.

Go, search her rugged mountain sides,
Her banks and braes so fair,

On sunny slope, on lonely moor,
   Her emblem Flower is there!

See! where it rears its haughty head—
   True Scot that ne'er will yield—
The Thistle! with its ruby crown,
   Stands monarch of the field.

It spreads those warlike arms about,
   To guard the land from spoil;
What foeman's foot e'er rested long
   On Caledonia's soil!

The banners of the Northern race
   Oft waved above its spears,
When Border shout and pibroch note
   Rang in the Southron ears.

O! Sons of Scotland! love it well,
   Your sires its virtues knew;
Be like your Thistle to the end,
   As staunch, as leal and true!

LIA FAIL,

The Scottish Stone of Destiny.

(See Note 5.)

WEIRD and mystic is the story
  Shrouded in forgotten lore,
How the Royal Stone of Scotland
  Found a place on Scotland's shore.

No human hands e'er fashioned it,
  Nor shaped its rugged form;
It thundered down the mountain side,
  Dislodged by Alpine storm.

59

'Twas pillow for the weary head
    At Bethel on the night
When Jacob's raptured vision saw
    The ladder crowned with light.

A thousand years passed o'er it
    In many climes and lands—
The throne of savage princes,
    Who ruled their heathen bands.

Ere the Assyrian hosts were shattered,
    Sleeping all the sleep of death,
Smitten in their battle harness,
    Blasted by the angel's breath;

Ere the star of Rome had risen
    Glorious after many wars,
Ere she first was led to battle
    By the wolf-nursed son of Mars;

The southern breeze blew softly,
    And filled the Spanish sail,

That bore to Erin's monarch
　The mystic Lia Fail.

Great Fergus seized the trophy,
　And on it, by God's grace,
Was crowned in bonnie Scotland
　First prince of Scottish race.

O'er a long line of heroes—
　Old Caledonia's kings,
The sacred Stone of Destiny
　A mystic glory flings.

And now the Royal City
　On Thames' historic shore
Enshrines the throne of Fergus,
　The Lia Fail of yore.

NOTES.

Note 1.

THE CANADIAN SONG SPARROW.

(Page 16.)

Every resident in the northern and eastern counties of the Dominion has heard the note of the song sparrow in all the woods and fields through the early days of spring. While his voice is familiar to the ear, very few can boast of having seen him, so carefully does he conceal himself from view. He dwells long upon his first and second notes, and, in metrical phrase, he forms a distinct "spondee." He then rattles off at least three "dactyls" in quick succession. In different localities different words are supplied to his music. Early settlers heard him echoing their despair with "Hard times in Canada, Canada, Canada." Others maintain that he is searching for traces of a dark crime, and unceasingly demands to know "Who killed Kennedy, Kennedy, Kennedy?" The thrifty farmer detects the words of warning—"Come now, sow-the-wheat, sow-the-wheat, sow-the-wheat." The writer has distinctly recognized in the little song the melancholy sentiments indicated in these lines.

Note 2.

UN CANADIEN ERRANT.

(Page 20.)

This well-known song was composed by the late A. Gérin-Lajoie shortly after the Rebellion of 1837, when so many

62

French-Canadians were in exile, "bannis de leurs foyers." Written to an old French air, its simple but touching words have given it an extraordinary popularity in the Province of Quebec.

NOTE 3.

THE GREAT DIVIDE.

(Page 33.)

Stephen, a station on the Canadian Pacific Railway, marks the summit of the Rocky Mountains. Here all trains are delayed to allow passengers to see the exact spot where the waters of a mountain spring divide, and overflow towards both the east and the west. These divided drops flow in opposite directions and by devious courses, and after descending more than 5,000 feet, they reach the sea levels of the Atlantic or the Pacific.

NOTE 4.

THE WHITE STONE CANOE.

(Page 34.)

The works of Schoolcraft contain many beautiful Indian legends, some of which, Longfellow tells us, he wove into his "Song of Hiawatha." "The White Stone Canoe" is one which he did not so immortalize, though it possesses great interest, and is rich in poetry and curious traditions. He made use of one of its incidents, however, where Chibiabos

> "In the Stone Canoe was carried
> To the Islands of the Blessed,
> To the land of Ghosts and Shadows."

In my treatment of the story I have naturally fallen into the simple metre, which the great American poet adopted as most suitable for Songs of the Forest and Tales of the Wigwam.

NOTE 5.

LIA FAIL,

The Scottish Stone of Destiny.

(Page 59.)

The *Lia Fail*, or Stone of Destiny, is the subject of many fabulous traditions. Ancient chronicles recount that, after having been Jacob's pillow at Bethel, it was a valued relic in the time of Gathelus, a Spanish king, and contemporary of Romulus. This monarch sent it with his son when the latter invaded Ireland. It was for centuries the coronation throne of Irish princes, until it was removed first to Iona, where Fergus, son of Erc, was crowned upon it, A.D. 503, and thence to Scone, in 842, by Kenneth II., when the Scots had overcome the Picts. It remained in the Abbey of Scone as the coronation chair of the kings of Scotland, until carried off by Edward I., in order that nothing might be left to remind the Scots of their former independence. He, however, placed it, with veneration, near the altar in Westminster Abbey, where it may now be seen, forming the support of the coronation chair of the British sovereigns. The mysterious connection which this stone is supposed to have with the destinies of the Scots is celebrated in the well known Latin couplet:—

> "Ni fallat fatum, Scoti quocunque locatum
> Invenient lapidem, regnare tenentur ibidem."

It was not unnatural that the accession of the Stuarts to the throne of Great Britain should have been hailed by many as the accomplishment of this singular prophecy.